Little Miss Upside Down

CAROLYN BRADLEY
Illustrated by: GENNEL MARIE SOLLANO

To order additional copies of this book, contact:
Xlibris
844-714-8691
www.Xlibris.com
Orders@Xlibris.com

ISBN: 978-1-6698-5501-9 (sc)
ISBN: 978-1-6698-5502-6 (e)

Print information available on the last page

Rev. date: 11/07/2022

To all children, everywhere, to keep
a dream in your heart.

A toyshop stood at the end of a long narrow street, in a very little town, a long time ago. The toyshop was painted white with blue flower boxes under each window. When the door was opened, three brass bells announced the news that a customer had entered.

The owner of the shop was a man whose name was Nathaniel. He took care of the toys with a loving and gentle hand. Nathaniel had grey hair and a grey mustache, and kindly blue eyes that showed that he cared for all.

In the toyshop were dolls of all different kinds
and sizes. In the evening, when the owner would
close the wooden door to go home, a very
unusual thing would happen. As soon as the
door was closed, all of the dolls suddenly came
to life. Sounds of chatter and great laughter
filled the air as they talked about all the things
that had happened in the store that day.

Liza, the little rag doll in the store, had reddish brown hair, brown eyes, and cheeks as rosy as a bright red apple. Her nose, however, had been mistakenly painted upside down. She had a fun-filled heart and was always making everyone feel good with her cheery ways. She wore a red dress with polka dots and bright blue shoes. Liza loved to play games in the store like jacks, jump rope and board games.

Margaret was dressed in a gown of yellow silk and had a beautiful jeweled crown on her long golden hair. She enjoyed sitting at the toy vanity with the oval mirror and playing with pretend doll make-up. Her manner was, however, very cross and unkind. She had even decided to call Liza, the little rag doll, "Little Miss Upside Down" because of her upside down nose. When she did, Liza only smiled, at her, and when she smiled, her nose looked more upside down than ever

One of the dolls was Megan, who was wearing a pink dress and had pink ribbons softly tucked in her long brown hair. A silver locket was around her neck that opened and closed. Her sparkly brown eyes caught your attention, as you could see the kindness and love in them. Megan enjoyed reading the wonderful books on the shelves, and the dolls would gather around her as she would read them the stories. Princesses and knights on beautiful horses, and kings and queens and children playing wonderful games came alive on the pages and in the dreams of the little dolls.

Another doll was Rachel who had long blonde hair and grey-blue eyes and who had skin as soft as a satin pillow. She wore a rose-dotted dress, with pink ballerina -like slippers on her feet with long pink ties. A white pearl bracelet was on her wrist. She had a loving heart and enjoyed drawing and painting beautiful pictures of the children who came into the store and who were so excited to see the dolls .She would also draw pictures of the snow falling outside the toy shop windows in the winter and the sun shining on the flowers in the blue window boxes in the summer.

Another doll was Laura, with eyes like deep blue water, and who was dressed all in blue to match her eyes. She had a soft sweet smile that showed her love and care for others. Laura loved watching the beautiful birds that flew past the toy shop windows and alighted on the window boxes of the store. She kept a little notebook, describing them all, and marveled at their beautiful colors, while listening to their beautiful songs.

Now all of the other dolls got along quite well with one another. Every evening they would have a tea party, with make-believe tea of course, and there just happened to be the right number of chairs for the little toy table in the store. Then they played games, each doll being careful to keep herself tidy and neat so as not to ruin her lovely clothes.

All of the dolls had dreams of being chosen
by nice little children who would take
them home and love them always.

Little Miss Upside Down dreamed most of all.

She thought she might never be chosen, because of her upside down nose. To make matters worse, Margaret made her even more doubtful of her ever being chosen, by always making fun of her upside down nose.

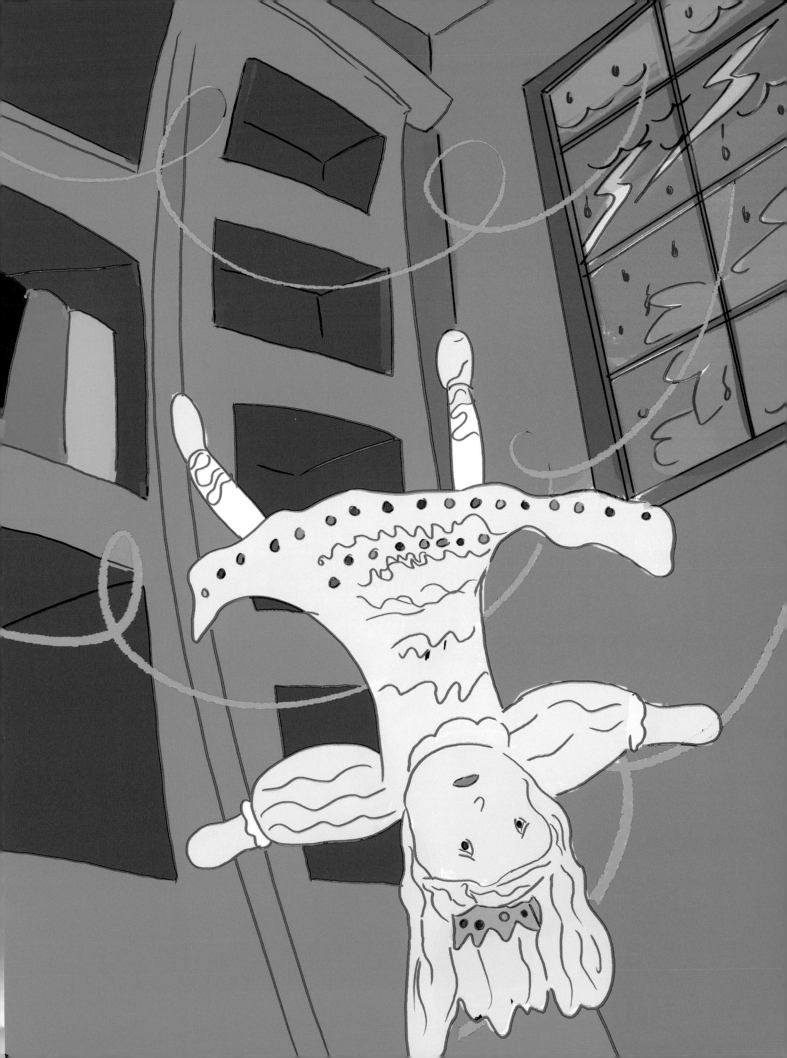

Now, one evening, when the shopkeeper left the store, he did not notice that one of the windows was still open. Of all nights for this to happen, a storm arose in the sky. Soon great drops of rain had begun to fall, and a howling wind roared through the little town, across the narrow street, and through the open window of the store.

Margaret, whose place was on the very top shelf, noticed the shelf beginning to sway. Much to her dismay, she felt herself toppling from the shelf, and down onto the floor. She landed with a thud on the hard floor. A long crack appeared down the side of her face.

The other dolls, though shaken by the wind, were not damaged. All of them immediately gathered around Margaret, to see if they could help.

"Oh dear," Margaret cried, "what happened to me?" The dolls did not want to tell Margaret, but she saw her reflection in the vanity mirror of the pink dressing table.

"I am not beautiful, anymore," she cried, and large doll tears rolled down her cracked face.

"Don't worry, Margaret," said Little Miss Upside Down, "perhaps the shopkeeper can mend your face with a little paste or glue."

"No, I don't think so," said Margaret. "I won't be beautiful ever again. No one will ever choose me now."

"I probably won't be chosen either, because of my upside down nose," said Little Miss Upside Down, "so we can play together and always be friends."

"Do you mean that you wouldn't laugh at me, like I laughed at you?" asked Margaret. 'You would really be my friend, always?"

Little Miss Upside Down said "Yes", and from that day on they became the best of friends.

The next morning the shopkeeper saw how Margaret had been damaged by the storm.

"Oh dear," he thought, "no one will ever buy her now, and it is in a place that cannot be mended. To make room for the new dolls that I will have to order, I think I will take Margaret and the little rag doll with the upside down nose to the children who are sick at the hospital tomorrow morning.

That evening, the dolls gave a farewell party for Liza and Margaret. They sat around the toy table on the toy chairs and talked about all of the fun they had had in the toyshop. Margaret apologized to all of the dolls for being so unkind and forgiveness was granted.

Megan reached up for her silver locket and unclasped it and placed it in the hand of Margaret as a farewell gift, saying,

"Margaret, When you learn to love, love comes in your heart and stays ·just like this locket. it can remind you of all the love that is kept safe in your heart."

Rachel slid her pearl bracelet off her wrist and gave it to Liza, likewise, as a remembrance of their friendship, saying,

"Liza, You have always been so kind and loving. You have made our days so cheerful and bright."

Laura took out two of the pictures of the beautiful
birds she had drawn in her notebook and signed
them with the words - "With love, from Laura"

"Oh, thank you, thank you all so much!" both
Liza and Margaret cried out as little tears
of happiness rolled down their cheeks.

Hugs and loving wishes were given
then, and a promise always to be friends
no matter where they were.

The next morning Margaret and Liza
found themselves in a wicker basket being
taken to the children at the hospital.

A nurse, named Betty, in a white starched uniform,
carefully lifted the two dolls from the basket.

"These will be perfect," she told the shopkeeper,
as she examined each doll carefully.

"The children that come here need mending in
many different ways. They will give these dolls
much love and care, in our playroom, while the
dolls will be able to show the children that
we all may need mending from time to time,
and that we are loveable, no matter what. I
know that they will be loved VERY much."

Two little girls, dressed in their night gowns ran over to the nurse, and they both exclaimed,

"Oh LOOK, HOW BEAUTIFUL they are!"

As the nurse turned to look at the shopkeeper, she didn't see the wink Margaret gave LIZA, as LIZA smiled her biggest smile yet!

Printed in the United States
by Baker & Taylor Publisher Services